This Rising Moon
book belongs to:

_____

Farmer McPeepers
and His Missing Milk Cows

by Katy S. Duffield

illustrated by
Steve Gray

rising moon

www.northlandpub.com

Composed in the United States of America
Printed in Hong Kong

Edited by Theresa Howell
Art Direction by David Jenney
Production Design by Rudy Ramos
Production supervised by Donna Boyd

FIRST IMPRESSION 2003
ISBN 0-87358-825-8

07 06 05 04 03   5 4 3 2 1

Library of Congress Cataloging-in-Publication Data

Duffield, Katy.
    Farmer McPeepers and his missing milk cows / by Katy Duffield ; illustrated by
Steve Gray.
        p. cm.
    Summary: A crafty herd of cows borrows Farmer McPeepers' eyeglasses so that they
can have a day on the town.
    [1. Cows—Fiction. 2. People with visual disabilities—Fiction. 3. Farm life—Fiction.
    4. Humorous stories.] I. Gray, Steve, ill. II. Title.

    PZ7.D87805 Far 2003   [E]—dc21

2002068272

To the loves of my life, Randy and Blake.
—K. S. D.

To Cindy Morningstar for making life fun.
—S. G.

Late one summer's evening on Farmer McPeepers' farm, the milk cows were up to no good.

At sunrise the next morning, Farmer McPeepers dragged himself out of bed, strolled over to the window, and squinted across the pasture.

"Good heavens!" he cried. "Where in the world are my milk cows?"

Lickity split, Farmer McPeepers threw open the screen door and rushed across the yard.

"Farmer!" Mrs. McPeepers called after him. "Don't forget your glasses! You know you can't see a thing without them."

But it was no use. Farmer McPeepers was already at the barn.

"Hold still, Thunderbolt," Farmer McPeepers said as he tightened the saddle on his trusty steed. "What's gotten into you, fella?"

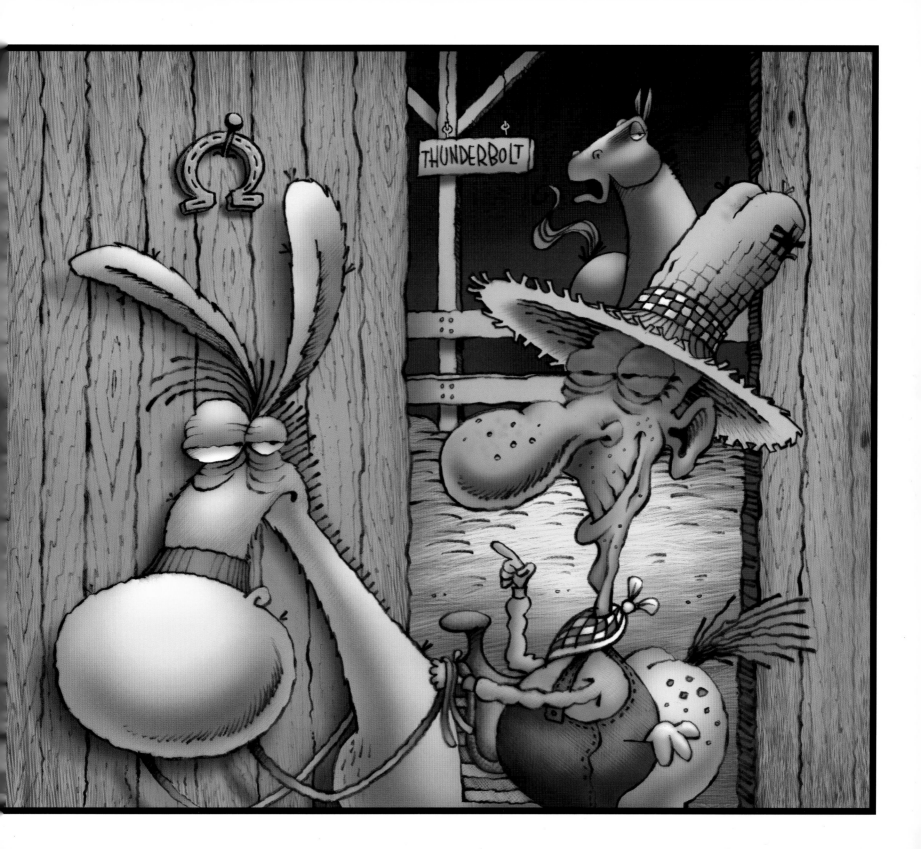

Farmer McPeepers and his mount clip-clopped up the road past Meyer's Pond. A rowboat filled with fishermen bobbed in the water.

Up and down. Down and up.

But Farmer McPeepers didn't see his milk cows.

A little farther along, Farmer McPeepers came upon some young 'uns swinging on a rope. He heard, "*Waahoo!*" and then *Splash!* as they dropped into the swimming hole. But Farmer McPeepers didn't see his milk cows.

"Good heavens!" he cried. "Where in the world are my milk cows?"

When he passed a park at the town's edge, a jumper skipped a double Dutch rope while climbers swung from jungle gym bars.

Someone smiled and waved, "Howdy-do, Farmer!"

Farmer nodded and waved, but still no milk cows.

When Farmer reached the town square, a long line
of moviegoers snaked its way down the sidewalk.
Farmer McPeepers smelled popcorn popping and hot
dogs roasting, but he didn't see his milk cows.

"Good heavens!" he cried. "Where in the world are
my milk cows?"

Farmer McPeepers continued on his way until he reached the school yard. Skateboarders swished by, while soccer players dribbled and dropkicked. Colorful kites fluttered in the breeze, but Farmer McPeepers didn't see his milk cows.

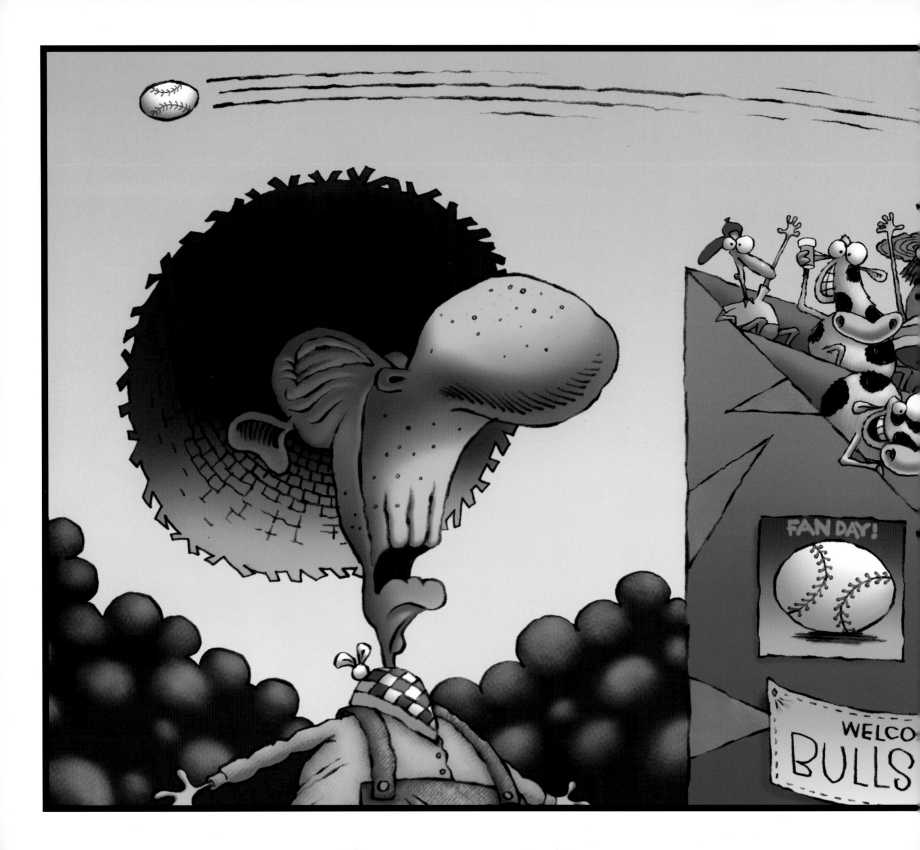

As Farmer McPeepers headed out of town, fans cheering for the home team filled the ballpark's bleachers. Farmer McPeepers heard the crack of the bat, but he didn't see his milk cows.

"Good heavens!" he cried. "Where in the world are my milk cows?"

A barn dance commenced at neighbor Nettleton's. The fiddler played while the square dance caller sang out, "Swing your partner. Do-si-do." It was quite a shindig, but Farmer McPeepers *still* didn't see his milk cows.

"Good heavens!" he cried. "I'm never going to find my milk cows."

Farmer McPeepers rode across the yard until he reached the barn. "Hold still, Thunderbolt," he said as he loosened the saddle. "What's gotten into you, fella?"

Just then, Farmer McPeepers noticed something shining on the chopping block.

"Well, looky there!" Farmer said. "My glasses!"

Late one summer's evening on Farmer McPeepers' farm, the milk cows were up to no good.